Odd Critters

By Sarah Forrest

No part of this publication may be reproduced without written permission of the publisher.

Second Edition 2022
Printed in the United Kingdom.
ISBN: 978-1-911151-21-0

© All Aboard Learning 2022
All Aboard Learning Ltd, 267 Banbury Road, Oxford OX2 7HT, UK
AllAboardLearning.com
This book is compatible with All Aboard Phonics UK Editions.

All Aboard Phonics Phase 5
Unit 1 Week 4

Week 1	ay, ou, ie, ea, Mr, Mrs, Ms
Week 2	oy, ir, ue, aw, there, people, oh, their
Week 3	wh, ew, oe, looked, asked, called
Week 4	au, ey, i_e, o_e, could, should, would
Week 5	a_e, u_e, e_e, ph
Week 6	Assessment week

All Aboard Phonics decodable books have a carefully controlled vocabulary and are specifically designed for children who are learning to read and write with All Aboard Phonics, or beginner readers learning at home.

Please take a moment to revise what phoneme (sound) is normally represented by each of these graphemes (letters). It is fine to help the learner if they are not sure.

au ey

i_e o_e

could should would

Pig-deers are pigs with tusks that curl up high. They could die if the tusks get too long.

The key trick is to trim their tusks, to stop them stabbing their skull.

The star-nose mole cannot see a thing. However, its cool nose can smell if it dives in a river.

It smells out insects and little fish to hunt in river valleys. It is the quickest eater too!

The komondor is a dog that should get some coat brushing each morning!

Its job is to keep sheep safe on farm hills and valleys. It will launch an attack if need be.

Its thick hair helps to keep off chills in the white winters.

Its coat helps the dog defend itself too. Attackers cannot bite all that hair.

Hairless cats feel soft, but have no fur. People have bred them to be like that.

Without fur, they could get a bad burn in the sunshine.

They should have cat sunscreen or a shirt. It would be quite a sight!

Image Credits:

Photo 1: Photo 193333050 © Craig Russell | Dreamstime.com

Photo 2: Photo 193333047 © Craig Russell | Dreamstime.com

Photo 3: ID: 1080387398 © Agnieszka Bacal

Photo 4: ID: 1126988069 © Agnieszka Bacal

Photo 5: Photo 169897162 © Slowmotiongli | Dreamstime.com

Photo 6: Photo 137672798 © Helena Cadanova | Dreamstime.com

Photo 7: Photo 131468704 © Helena Cadanova | Dreamstime.com

Photo 8: Photo 32346025 © Lovasz | Dreamstime.com

Photo 9: Photo 50647676 / Cat © Cynoclub | Dreamstime.com

Photo 10: Photo 12127533 / Cat © Natalia Belotelova | Dreamstime.com

Photo 11: Photo 50647709 / Cat © Cynoclub | Dreamstime.com